THE GYM TEACHER FROM THE BLACK LAGOON

STORY BY
MIKE THALER

PICTURES BY
JARED LEE

Cartwheel
B·O·O·K·S ®

SCHOLASTIC INC.

New York   Toronto   London   Auckland   Sydney
Mexico City   New Delhi   Hong Kong   Buenos Aires

For Alan Boyko, a friend indeed!
—M.T.

To my big brother, whose first name rhymes with gym.
—J.L.

Visit us at www.abdopublishing.com Reinforced library bound edition published in 2011 by Spotlight, a division of ABDO Publishing Group, 8000 West 78th Street, Edina, Minnesota 55439. This edition was reprinted by permission of Scholastic Inc. No part of this publication may be reprinted in whole or in part, or in any form or by any means, electronic or mechanical, without written permission of the publisher. For information regarding permission, write to Scholastic Inc., Attention: Permissions Department, 557 Broadway, New York, NY 10012.

Printed in the United States of America, Melrose Park, Illinois.
082010
012011

 This book contains at least 10% recycled materials.

Library of Congress Cataloging-in-Publication Data
This title was previously cataloged with the following information:
Thaler, Mike, 1936-,
 The gym teacher from the black lagoon / by Mike Thaler ; pictures by Jared Lee.
    p. cm.
 [1. Physical education and training–Fiction. 2. Schools–Fiction. 3. Humorous Stories.] I. Lee, Jared D., ill. II. Title.
PZ7.T3 Gy 1994
 [E]–dc20   96171888

ISBN: 978-1-59961-794-7 (reinforced library bound edition)

All Spotlight books have reinforced library binding and are
manufactured in the United States of America.

We're getting a new gym teacher this year.

He's coming over from the Junior High.
His name is *Mr. Green*!

The kids say he's big, he's mean,
he's rarely seen.

They say he's *very* hairy,
and his knuckles touch the ground.

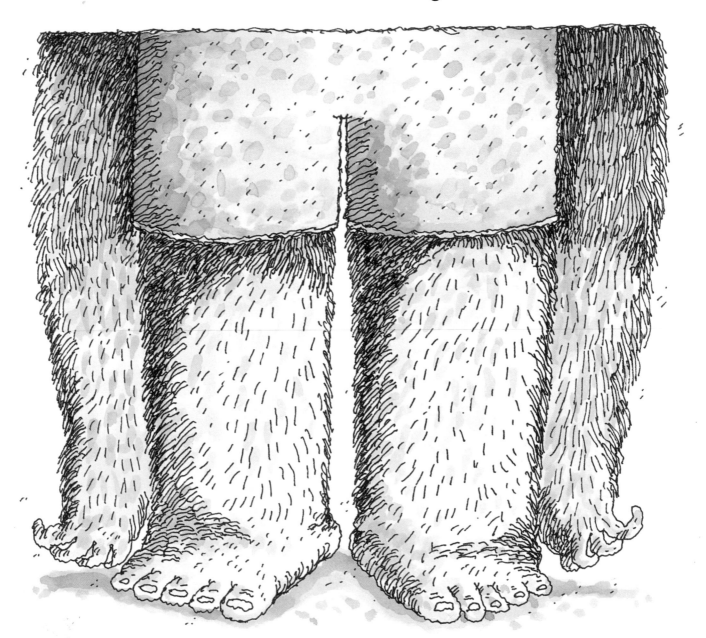

His nickname is COACH KONG
and no one has actually heard him speak any words.

He just blows his whistle a lot.

They say he has a little office
full of balls and clubs and tires.

The big kids say he makes you run a lot.
First a lap around the gym.

Then a lap around the school.

Then a lap around the world!

Then he gives you fitness tests.
You have to lift his pickup truck over your head
before the semester ends.
I guess that's why they call it a "pickup" truck.

You spend a lot of time getting in shape.
He makes you do push-ups, pull-ups,
chin-ups, and sit-ups.
But most of the kids just do *throw-ups*.

Then you have to climb THE ROPE.
If you don't reach the top, he sets the bottom on fire!

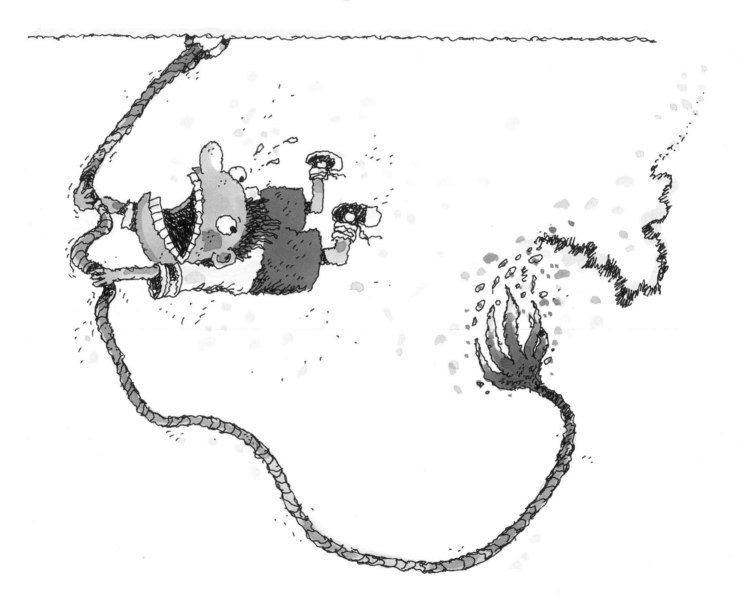

They say there are still kids up in the ceiling
of the Junior High gym.

If you don't pass the fitness tests,
your body is *donated* to science.

Then there's the posture test.
If you don't pass that, he ties you between two boards.

But there are games, too.
He makes you play DODGE ball...

with his truck!

And TAG with Crazy Glue...

And baseball with real bats!

Then there's THE PARACHUTE!
He has us all hold on tight to the side
and jump out of an airplane.

He's also big on gymnastics.
He makes you walk "the beam"

and jump over "the horse."

He makes you do

HANDSTANDS,

HEADSTANDS,

NOSE STANDS,

and MUSIC STANDS.

He makes you do SOMERSAULTS

and CARTWHEELS.

But the worst thing is SQUARE DANCING... with the *girls*!

Oh, oh! There's his whistle!
I better go line up.

"Hi, kids. I'm Mr. Green, your new gym teacher."
I can't believe it! He's a regular guy!

"Let's play some basketball," says Mr. Green.
We do, and I score two baskets.

This is great!
I'm going to like gym.